ALI
THE
GREAT

and the Paper Airplane Flop

by SAADIA FARUQI   illustrated by DEBBY RAHMALIA

PICTURE WINDOW BOOKS
a capstone imprint

For Adam —SF
For Alesha —DR

Published by Picture Window Books, an imprint of Capstone
1710 Roe Crest Drive
North Mankato, Minnesota 56003
capstonepub.com

Library of Congress Cataloging-in-Publication Data
Names: Faruqi, Saadia, author. | Rahmalia, Debby, illustrator.
Title: Ali the Great and the paper airplane flop / written by Saadia Faruqi; illustrated by Debby Rahmalia.
Description: North Mankato, Minnesota : Picture Window Books, an imprint of Capstone, 2023. | Series: Ali the Great | Audience: Ages 5 to 8. | Audience: Grades K-1. | Summary: On a rainy day at recess, second grader Ali Tahir teaches his classmates to make and fly paper airplanes, but when they have a contest to see whose plane can fly farthest, Ali is disappointed by the results of his throw. Includes instructions on making paper airplanes.
Identifiers: LCCN 2022048880 (print) | LCCN 2022048881 (ebook) | ISBN 9781666393903 (hardcover) | ISBN 9781484681312 (paperback) | ISBN 9781484681329 (pdf) | ISBN 9781484687536 (kindle edition) | ISBN 9781484681343 (epub)
Subjects: LCSH: Pakistani Americans—Juvenile fiction. | Paper airplanes—Juvenile fiction. | Friendship—Juvenile fiction. | CYAC: Pakistani Americans—Fiction. | Paper airplanes—Fiction. | Friendship—Fiction.
Classification: LCC PZ7.1.F373 Alk 2023 (print) | LCC PZ7.1.F373 (ebook) | DDC 813.6 [Fic]—dc23/eng/20221115
LC record available at https://lccn.loc.gov/2022048880
LC ebook record available at https://lccn.loc.gov/2022048881

Designers: Kay Fraser and Tracy Davies

Printed and bound in China. 5378

TABLE OF CONTENTS

I'M ALi TahiR,
aLSo KNOWN AS

ALI
THE
GREAT!

And this is My faMiLy...

ABBA
doctoR

AMMA
scientist

DADA
chief joke teLLeR

DADI
best cook in
the WoRLd

FATEH
sneaky LittLe bRotheR

LET'S LEARN SOME URDU!

Ali and his family speak both English and Urdu, a language from Pakistan. Now you'll know some Urdu too!

ABBA (ah-BAH)—father (also baba)

AMMA (ah-MAH)—mother (also mama)

BHAI (BHA-ee)—brother

DADA (DAH-dah)—grandfather on father's side

DADI (DAH-dee)—grandmother on father's side

SALAAM (sah-LAHM)—hello

SHUKRIYA (shuh-KREE-yuh)—thank you

Chapter 1

BORED

It was raining outside. Ali's class was stuck in the gym for recess.

"I'm so bored!" Ali groaned.

"Yeah," Zack agreed. "There's nothing to do inside!"

Yasmin saw some boxes and peeked inside. "Ooh, art supplies!" she said. She took out some paper and crayons and started coloring.

Ali thought coloring was boring. He watched Yasmin work. Was there something fun he could do with that paper?

"I know!" Ali suddenly
shouted. "Let's make paper
airplanes!"

Yasmin looked up and
frowned. "I don't know how."

Ali grinned. "Don't worry," he said. "I'll help you. I'm an expert!"

He took a piece of paper and folded it carefully. Once, twice, three times. He made sure the creases were very sharp.

Ta-da! Ali held up his paper
airplane.

"Cool!" Zack said. "Can you
please make me one too?"

"Me too!" said Emma.

Chapter 2
THE CONTEST

Ali took more papers from the

box and folded more airplanes.

He didn't rush. He had to be

careful and neat. If he made a

mistake, the airplane wouldn't

fly as far.

Soon, there was a pile of airplanes for his friends to choose from.

Yasmin grabbed her crayons.
"I'm going make a design on
mine!" she said.

"Great idea!" Ali replied. Art
wasn't boring when there were
planes involved!

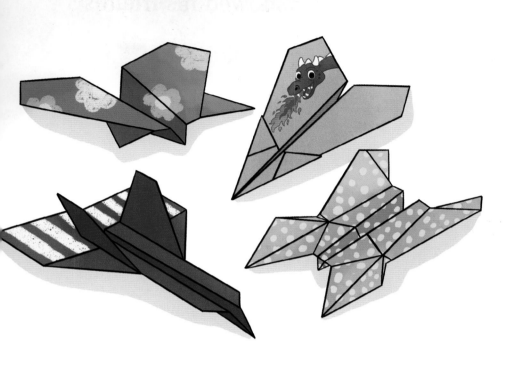

Ali added white racing stripes
to his. Yasmin drew flowers on
hers. Emma's had polka dots.
Zack's had a fire-breathing
dragon!

Then Ali showed his friends how to fly their planes.

"You have to hold up your plane like this and lean forward," he said. "And you have to throw hard."

"Let's have a contest!" Zack
suggested. "Whoever's plane flies
the farthest wins!"

"Okay!" Ali said. He was the
pro, and he was ready!

Emma went first. Her plane

flew toward the basketball hoop.

"Yay!" she said.

Then it was Zack's turn. His

plane went even farther. "Beat

that!" Zack said.

Yasmin was third. She smiled

nervously.

"You can do it, Yasmin!" Ali

cheered.

Yasmin aimed carefully then threw. Her plane landed all the way in the bleachers! "Wow!" everyone cried.

CHaPteR 3

AND THE WINNER IS . . .

Finally, it was Ali's turn. He wasn't worried. He built the best airplanes. He would definitely win!

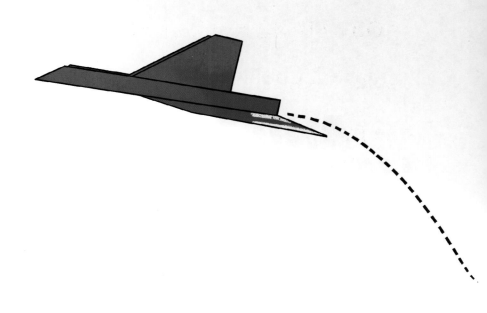

Ali threw his paper airplane with all his might. It soared high up. Then it dipped down. Then it looped and twisted!

Everyone watched the airplane. It looped once more. Then it landed . . . right behind Ali.

"Oh no!" Ali cried. This was terrible. He wasn't the winner. He came in last!

"I lost?" he said, surprised.

"No, you didn't, Ali," Yasmin said. "You're the winner, with me!"

"I am?" Ali asked.

Emma nodded. "She's right! You made our airplanes for us," she said.

"And you taught us the best way to fly," Zack added.

Ali started to feel better. He *did* know the most about building paper airplanes.

Yasmin clapped. "We both win!" she cheered loudly.

"Teamwork!" Zack said, even louder.

Ali pointed to the box of supplies. "Ready for another round?" he asked.

"Bring it on, co-pilot!" Yasmin replied.

JUST JOKING AROUND

How do rabbits travel?
By hare-plane

Why did the airplane get sent to its room?
Because it had a bad altitude

Why did the teenager study on an airplane?
Because he wanted a higher education

What happens if you wear a watch on an airplane?
Time flies!

BUILD A PAPER AIRPLANE

Take a sheet of paper and follow these directions to make a paper airplane like Ali!

THINK **BIG** WITH **ALI THE GREAT!**

☆ Ali is frustrated that he doesn't win the paper airplane contest, even though he built all the planes. Can you relate to how Ali feels? How do you help yourself feel better when something seems unfair?

☆ Co-pilots are people who share the work and responsibility of flying a plane. The word "co-pilot" can also mean partner in a project or adventure. Think of a project or activity you would like to try. Who would you choose as your co-pilot, and why?

☆ About the AuthoR ☆

Saadia Faruqi is a Pakistani American writer, interfaith activist, and cultural sensitivity trainer featured in *O, The Oprah Magazine*. Author of the Yasmin chapter book series, Saadia also writes middle grade novels, such as *Yusuf Azeem Is Not a Hero*, and other books for children. Saadia is editor-in-chief of *Blue Minaret*, an online magazine of poetry, short stories, and art. Besides writing, she also loves reading, binge-watching her favorite shows, and taking naps. She lives in Houston with her family.

☆ About the ILLusTRAtoR ☆

Debby Rahmalia is an illustrator based in Indonesia with a passion for storytelling. She enjoys creating diverse works that showcase an array of cultures and people. Debby's long-term dream was to become an illustrator. She was encouraged to pursue her dream after she had her first baby and has been illustrating ever since. When she's not drawing, she spends her time reading the books she illustrated to her daughter or wandering around the neighborhood with her.

JOIN

ALI THE GREAT

ON His Adventures!

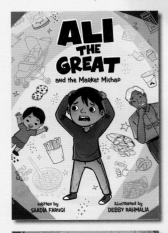